Return To
Innocence

Faye Dumas-Harrison

Unless otherwise noted, all Scripture quotations are from the King James Version (KJV) from the Holy Bible.

Published by:
Frankie Dumas-Harrison, LLC dba – Professional Outlook.net
P. O. Box 2494, Covington, GA   30015
www.professionaloutlook.net

ISBN: 978-0-578-76263-0

ACKNOWLEDGEMENTS

In sweet memory of my Aunt Deborah Jean Dumas.

I would like to thank God for blessing and keeping me in a positive state of mind and being the force and strength behind my ability to express myself through writing and creative design. I give him the glory and praise for it is his glory that I can share this creative gift, which he placed inside of me. Words will never articulate my love and desire to please you!

To my wonderful husband Clay Harrison thanks for loving me for 20 plus yrs. Thanks for the life lesson to learn to love myself again and to never lose yourself for no one only God. Know that I love you dearly and my love for you is indescribable. Thank you for always believing in me when I didn't believe in myself! For that you will always hold a special place in my heart.

To my children: Deonte, Joshua, Jana Dumas, Jayla Salazar, Taylor Harrison, Jazmyne Jordan and Jarquavious Hunt. All of you have my heart outside of my body...So make me proud of you! Remember Though you may have experienced some setbacks in this thing call life, know that it's not over until we all win!!!

Special thanks to: My mom Elder Carrie dumas and my spiritual mother and father Pastor Travis C. Jennings & Pastor Stephanie Jennings (Sister). I love all three of you dearly. You three are a great inspiration and mentor to me. Without your wisdom, guidance, teaching, and believing, none of this would be possible. For your guidance have been invaluable and have helped mold me and navigate the destiny of my life. I honor you and love you.

To my baby sister Sabrina Lawrence and my brother Timothy Dumas please know that God has a plan for all of us. Stay focused on your objectives and goals. Again, Sabrina I can't think you enough for loving me back to life when I wanted to give up...you will always be my bonus child (inside joke).

To my dad Frank Dumas don't think I could have left you out because without you I wouldn't be here today. Much love!!

To all my grandchildren – Make me proud of you! You all have come and took over my heart...don't tell your parents that you all have moved them and took their place...lol

Special gratitude: Special thanks for pushing me even when I didn't want to be push and for being there at a very low part of my life when I wanted to give up and let go of the towel...Again thank you so much for obeying God and being my ram in the bush...Prophetess Pamela Tucker...Love you for life!

To everyone I left out, I apologize, but I still got love for you! Charge it to my mind and not my heart!

And to my readers/supporters...THANK YOU FROM THE BOTTOM OF MY HEART!

CONTENTS

Chapter 1
In the beginning...THE FOUNDATION

Janiã – It was a dark raining Friday night. I can remember like it was yesterday as my two sisters Jaylnn, Jazzie, my mom, and I was standing at the bus stop in the rain eating fried chicken as we were waiting on the transit bus #451 to head to church. See church was Mommy Dukes life and anyone that was part of her world it became your life. It appears we were in church every day of the week. I remember standing at the bus stop thinking when I turn 18, I'm out. See we lived a sheltered life to the point Mommy dukes didn't allow her children to go anywhere but the church, school, and home and maybe occasionally, I got to spend the night at my play Aunt TT house. See back in the day anyone that grew up together became family and family back in the day always stuck together and had an unbreakable loyalty. As you notice I said I got to spend the night. I kind of felt bad for Jaylnn and Jazzie because as kids they never had a life. On this particular Friday night, I remember it so well because so much happened at service that night. See we attended a church called The Christ House of Truth it was a Pentecostal church. And yes, I was known as a Holy Roller as a child. We weren't allowed to wear pants, makeup, or God forbid come to church without sleeves on your shirt. If you broke any of those rules you were you were going straight to hell do not pass go and do not collect two hundred dollars. This night was the start of a new beginning for me, but I wouldn't realize it until years to come.

As we entered the church on this Friday night, I remember my cousin Nikki and I snuck out of the church to go down the street to the penny store to purchase candy for the crew. Yes, even at a young age we had cliques. And if you didn't belong to the clique then you were considered a nobody. See growing up I didn't know that there is a difference between church and kingdom. My cousin and I were well respected because our parents belonged to that inner circle that holiness churches or churches period don't like to admit exists. See somehow, we became the ring leaders by default. See these cliques or inner circle exists and they amplify each other's accomplishments and goals that are common beyond their circle. Upon sneaking back into the church because the ushers back in the day were mothers of Zion and didn't play nothing like these 21-century ushers that just stand at the door with matching colors and no power. They will snatch you up and dare your parent or parent parents to say something. As we were playing around and eating candy being children, we heard a loud noise. Mother B yelled to us get on your knees and just say JESUS, JESUS, JESUS, as fast as you can. Then she gave all the kids a bible to hold up to our hearts. Wasn't sure what was going on, but it seemed kind of scary. You see I was so noisy that I opened my eyes and started peeking trying to see what was going on. Once I opened my eyes and start saying JESUS, I wish I would have just obeyed. What I saw was unbelievable. There were this 90 lbs. lady throwing 200 to 300 hundred-pound men with one arm. As the Pastor was speaking to the lady and calling names which I'm sure wasn't hers that had me confused until I heard the lady with a male voice say loudly **"YOU DON'T SCARE ME"**! Then I heard someone say that the pastor was calling the demons by name and speaking to them. See things of this nature happened all the time where demons were cast out and people got healed and delivered for real on the spot. I'm talking about blind eyes being opened and people placing crutches, medicines and whatever had them bound at the altar and left it there. One thing for sure I didn't understand back then as a child that spirits lurk and look for an open vessel so that's why the ushers were true Mothers of Zion that wore the white gloves and keep their heads covered with a veil and I can say God gave them the gift and wisdom to protect the innocent and guard the gates of the church as a whole. They weren't just there to make sure the seats were filled for the camera and the show. The foundation was pure. Mothers of Zion had humility which is the solid foundation of all virtues. They had a genuine prayer life, they fasted and had faith, courage and they had a love for people and God...they didn't accept any and everything as if it was ok...they weren't afraid to tell the pastor or anyone else if something they did or said wasn't right before God. This taught me to obey those in authority over me. **Hebrews 13:17** ([17] Obey them that have the rule over you, and submit yourselves: for they watch for your souls, as they that must give account, that they may do it with joy, and not with grief: for that is unprofitable for you.)

Another thing I can say I learned that family is more than those born with the same DNA or that were raised in the same household. The church taught you a lot about unity and family when I was growing up. Even though I couldn't wait till I turned 18 I must say when one person ate everyone ate. No one was left out or felt lonely doing any holidays because everyone was always at someone's house from the church. Somehow after church on a giving Sunday a box of Church's Chicken feed over 3 to 4 families. To this day I still can't figure out how God made this possible. Reminds you of **Matthew 14:13-21** ([19] And he commanded the multitude to sit down on the grass, and took the five loaves, and the two fishes, and looking up to heaven, he blessed, and brake, and gave the loaves to his disciples, and the disciples to the multitude. [20] And they did all eat and were filled; and they took up of the fragments that reminded twelve baskets full. [21] And that they eaten were about five thousand men, beside women and children.) I can say we didn't have all the answers back then but one thing for sure The Body of Christ had love, faith, and a solid foundation. My life today got me so confused because I'm trying to figure out when did God's word change and what happened to the real hospital that a person could run to for deliverance and peace. The kind of peace that if you had to go to the hospital to see a doctor that you knew all is well b/c you had just left God's house and received confirmation. I remember a time that you would see a drunk person walking and about to pass a church they would cross the street b/c they felt convicted and out of respect for the church building and at the time there wasn't any service or event or anything going on. People need to honor God's house from the pulpit to the door as they use to.

I grew to learn religion is a specific set of organized beliefs and practices, usually shared by a community or group. Spirituality is more of an individual practice and has to do with having a sense of peace and purpose. It is also related to the process o developing beliefs around the meaning of life and connection with others and you obtain this from having a relationship with God. So, by saying this, I learned you must have a strong foundation to withstand the storms of life. Now I see why mom Dukes kept us in church and why it was important to have Praise and Worship to magnify God; And it was also important to hear the Word of God (^{17} So then Faith cometh by hearing, and hearing by the word of God.) **Romans 10:17**. And the third thing I learned a good foundation requires prayer and fasting. This will purify and cleanse the body and help release more of self. It's a denying of our carnal nature to fulfill the desires of God. (^{6} Is not this the fast that I have chosen? To lose the bands of wickedness, to undo the heavy burdens, and to let the oppressed go free, and that ye break every yoke?) **Isaiah 58:6.** So you see, we must be more than just familiar with the bible. The more time we spend in the Word, the more opportunity we have to grow in Christ, it makes it easier to trust and believe in God. And the most important benefit is God's word will give you spiritual and physical life to endure.

Ok now let's get back to this inner circle that no one wants to admit exist. This inner circle is supposed to be the people that the leaders trust and who will always be there when they need them and be what we call their advisers to keep them accountable. However, all I have seen and experienced with inner circles within a church have been toxic. It's just a group of friends that's close to leaders who enable the leader's sins and turn a blind eye to whatever is going on and in return, the leader makes sure they are well compensated or it's just a group of people that just look out for each other and themselves to make sure everyone connected to the circle is good. No one has any accountability. This made me want to turn away from going to church. My perception and I'm sticking to it!

"²⁹ If your right eye makes you stumble and leads you to sin, tear it out and throw it away [that is, remove yourself from the source of temptation]; for it is better for you to lose one of the parts of your body, than for your whole body to be thrown into hell". **Matthew 5:29 AMP.**

Jazzie – Growing up I can remember always having my way. Many called me spoiled because I always got my way. Even though I wasn't allowed to go to many places growing up, I remember enjoying life. The funniest part of growing up was staying in trouble with my older sister Jaylyn. The trouble I got into with her was well worth it now that I look back over life. The trouble brought me joy as well as taught me life lessons and how to survive in a cold world and all the rest I learned from going to church. I learned more from the church you can say. It taught many what and whatnots in life. See growing up in church I saw some of the best fights, arguments, bad habits, and many other things. I learned doing things in the name of God or for the church that people will turn a blind eye to. The church was the only place that a person can hang or stay out all night at another man or women's house and don't get questioned. The pastor, minister, deacon, and mainly the musicians can be cheating on their significant other and everyone in the church knows about it and it completely gets ignored. Now let anyone else get caught outside of their marriage and they get shamed from the pulpit. Now don't get me wrong it had some good experiences and life lessons as well. You can say the church help mold me. The foundation was real and taught me the true meaning of forgiveness, trust, and unity. So, with saying that my experiences and foundation in the church was social, fulfilling, and fun...with a little Jesus tossed in the mix. Because of this I received Christ but never reached the spiritual maturity that was I needed growing up.

Jaylnn – As I reflect on life and growing up, I can say that I lived a wonderful life. I had my mother, father, and two sisters. We had a nice home and nice things, so life I can say was great, so I thought. I enjoyed going to church and being a lead singer in the choir. I was well known and very popular at school. I was head of the cheerleader squad and class queen, what more can I ask for? Even though I was older than my baby sister by a year people thought that we were twins because we were together all the time. If you saw one you saw the other and growing up, we looked a lot alike. I can remember my family taking weekly trips to the park and annual vacations out of town because of me always bugging my dad. You can say I was a daddy's girl. Everyone seems to enjoy eating dinner together and the family trips except my oldest sister Janiã. I don't get it...why does she always want to be somewhere alone reading. I remember growing up she would sit in the same spot all day and only get up to go to the bathroom and check on me and my baby sister Jazzie. If we were good, happy, and safe, then she was good and happy. It's as if protecting us brought her joy. I think God put her here to protect us. You can say he blessed us with our own personal angel...She had an indescribable heart. She would save the world if she could.

I remember going to church all the time growing up, but my foundation was mainly family. Whether it was my biological family I was raised with or my family that was built within the church or simply my friends that were always around and became family. See the church taught me to have faith in myself, a higher power, and others in the communities that we build together. See the church that I grew up in didn't teach me to advocate for loving and healthy relationships between parents, siblings, and extended family. Any and everything was almost a secret. A lot of things that I joined or did in the church was because my friends or family did it or simply because I was told by someone of authority within the ministry. The foundation of my beliefs at the church that I was raised at had taught me that you couldn't ask why to those that had authority over you. I would later grow to realize that the basic of the biblical foundation was good but not the religious aspect of the house wasn't. My foundation taught me that holiness and living right is a lifestyle and a choice. But growing up my devotion to the church began to define me. So, I started doing right because my character was to do the right thing even if no one else does or if anyone has seen me, not because I thought it would change the world but because I refuse to be changed by the world.

[4] Abide in me, and I in you. As the branch cannot bear fruit of itself, except it abide in the vine, no more can ye, except ye abide in me. [15] I am the vine, ye are the branches: He that abideth in me, and I in him, the same bringeth forth much fruit: for without me ye can do nothing. **John 15:45.**

Chapter 2   What Drives Your Life

Jalynn – As I sit at home I'm thinking if people had a clue, they wouldn't always accept everyone just b/c they can quote scripture or give a word. Let me know when you accomplish how to make the principles of God's word work for you. If you don't accept all this junk in the secular world, I'm wondering why are we accepting it when it comes to our soul? It's so many weak-minded people nowadays that they believe anybody...how you keep listening to someone who has no wisdom, no stability, and covering & lack of knowledge. If they had wisdom, then they wouldn't be wondering...Get Real...you can read a word for yourself...Just saying...I mean week after week, day after day, and year after year. Do you mean God still hasn't come through yet? And we wonder why so many souls or lost and scared to trust God...Are you a good example? When people see you, do they see God? I'm asking myself these questions. I guess I'm thinking too much now my mind wanders to thinking about living in the **"POSSIBILITIES OF GOD"** ...I remember going to bible study and the message was Prevailing Plans! (Plans must be visualized, verbalized, and must have actions...It made me think of something I read that if events aren't planned, they seldom take place...Armies never go to battle without a plan. Coaches don't send players into a game without a plan. Chefs don't begin preparation for a great meal without a plan. So, you can't start down the road to success without a plan. So, write the vision and make it plain...Make SMART Goals (specific, measurable, attainable, realistic, and timely); ([37] For with God nothing shall be impossible.) **Luke 1:37.**

Jazzie – Well the saying is whatever you feed the most is what leads you. Many believe that circumstances are what drives your life. Life to me is about choices. It's your choice to be free. Freedom from anything starts with a conscious decision. The reality is that any cycle in your life can change with a choice. Once you make a choice to chose to be free your actions will follow, and you will see the shift in the direction of your life will take. You cannot go back in time and change the past, however; you do have the power to create your present...And from here this is how I started creating what I call my world. ([19] Behold, I will do a new thing, now it shall spring forth; shall ye not know it? I will even make a way in the wilderness, and rivers in the desert.) **Isaiah 43:19**.

Janiã – I came to realize that your past can control your future if you don't face it. We are products of our past, but we don't have to be a prisoner of it. Your past is just that the past! The past molestations hurt and whatever bad experience you have endured has to be dealt with or it will deal with you. Those who have hurt me in my past cannot continue to hurt me unless I hold onto the pain through resentment. I had to learn and heal from it, and let it go. ([18] Remember ye, not the former things, neither consider the things of old.) **Isaiah 43:18**. When I learned my God-given purpose is when my life started having meaning. Once you learn what your purpose in life is you will learn which battles are worth fighting and which battles should be ignored. My purpose gives me the foundation on which to base decisions and allocate my time and resources to learn to love and start living life.

Chapter 3   Living Life

Janiã   - I had become so numb to life b/c of this spin cycle of a merry-go-round I was stuck on and it wouldn't shut off. My heart and mind had become deprived of feelings. My heart had become hardend. I was unable to move and had become paralyzed to life. I can see the promises on the canvas, I heard the promises and I tried and wanted to believe the promises but all the faith in me was sucked out and I was drowning and didn't know how to reach, and grab hold again. The more I got ahead two steps I was knocked back eight. You are talking about a double…wow! It was to the point where I didn't want to pray anymore because I didn't know what to believe. So many things had hit me from those that shared my same last name and yes, some the same DNA that I was living to everyone else but dead mentally and spiritually to myself. The python was choking the very breath out of me. I was drowning and screaming **HELP I CAN'T BREATHE**! But no one could hear my cries! I was depressed and didn't even realize it. How can you be surrounded by so many people day by day and no one even realizes you, yourself the strong one needed just one person to be there for you. Someone that you could lean on and let it all out without judgment or condemnation. In this thing called life, it had caught up with me. The toll of being molested as a child, having children out of wedlock, having an abortion, a miscarriage, and the list goes on. Money, the big house, or the seven cars nothing could buy me happiness and give me the joy that I once had growing up. Just what could it be?

Jazzie – I'm living my life to the fullest. As I sit around and talk to my friends, I wonder how we got to this point and we go to church day after day and year after year. I discovered that many have no RELATIONSHIP with God! I discovered we grew up in church, but never grew in Christ. We know Hymns, But Don't know "HIM". I'm wondering can I say that I even have a relationship with him. My family and I faithful get up and go and serve at the church regularly so of course, I have a relationship with God because I'm over the minister of music at the church I attend right? But I'm wondering because if you name it yep, I did it. It didn't help that my husband and I were secretly part owners of a strip club/night lounge and yes, we pay our tithes faithfully our personal lives and for our business. I make sure that God gets his tenth off the top. I think the preacher knows but doesn't complain because it's so much money coming into the church that it helps him overlook that it's dirty money. The reason I even got into the business was seeing the dichotomy of my parents growing up from church **FACE to HOME LIFE** made me think is it all worth it or is everyone a hypocrite? Is God even real?

Jaylnn – I'm at a stage in my life that I enjoy being in ministry with my husband. People had finally accepted that I had married outside my race. So, what more can I ask for, my husband has just been ordained as a Prophet and we have one of the most thriving churches in our region and I had a very supportive family (my husband and children that is). I have my children by my side to travel with me to go visit this church to get a word from this Apostle and take what we learn back to our ministry to help keep our church growing and thriving. Sometimes we also went to this church that many were flocking to like flies to get a word from this Apostle. My husband loved to visit this church also because everyone knew if this man of God gave you a word that you can take it to the bank. It was the prophetic anointing that was on this Apostle's life and everyone couldn't deny that he walked heavily in his calling. You see a prophet's voice becomes the Oracle of God. **Deuteronomy 28: 1-3** (¹ And it shall come to pass, if thou shalt hearken diligently unto the voice of the Lord they God, to observe and to do all his commandments which I command thee this day, that the Lord thy God will set thee on high above all nations of the earth: ² And all these blessings shall come on thee, and overtake thee, if thou shalt hearken unto the voice of the Lord thy God. ³ Blessed shalt thou be in the city, and blessed shalt thou be in the field.) See when you have an Apostolic calling on your life you are to rebuke people. That is why the body of Christ had started operating in error because no one wants to rebuke anyone anymore. You see we never intended on being this megachurch, our goal was to just be an effective church. I liked the fact that this minister's heart was pure. Being in his presence you can feel God and

I prayed that his heart stayed that way. I knew growing up that God gave preachers a certain level and type of charisma. But I have seen so many ministers/pastors had fallen because the Godly charisma is powerful and because they weren't being properly covered the flesh crept in and the power got to them. So, my goal in life was to please God and make sure I keep my husband's heart pure as he followed God and help guard it in prayer. My husband spirit reminded me of the spirit of this Apostle so much that I also kept this Apostle in prayer because he was a true General in the body of Christ and much needed and I didn't want him to turn into one of these prosperity preachers that can't or won't give a word unless you giving a seed. I was glad that they not only prophesied, but they didn't look at a person's sin or spiritual immaturity, instead, they looked and judged a person on the God in the person where they see them at spiritually in their future and not their present state.

Even though I had stopped going around my family it wasn't because I didn't love them, but it was because it was some experiences and lessons that God was trying to teach me so that I wouldn't be leaning on my family or anything that was familiar and would be a hindrance to my lessons that I need to learn to be a witness and help God's people for me to become the person he wanted and created me to be. The funny part I don't even know when the wedge and separation crept up between my family because we were such a tight family, but I do know a division was there. It took years to learn that whatever caused that it was God's plan.

Chapter 4   The Reason for Everything

Janiã – As I was sitting in my living room starring out the window late one night...I was asleep but woke. It was as if I could see God in the sky in my window and it was as if he was looking down through my window and crying. It was so vivid that I felt as if I could reach up and wipe the tears away. Then within a couple of days, something had hit the land that everyone wasn't prepared for. Spiritual leaders, nor doctors (in a real hospital), not even certified counselors. Because of people's greed and the church had taped over into a religious and worldly state the body of Christ was divided, and people were hurting and no hospital to turn to. Those that God called to be a shepherd was bleeding on the sheep. Then others were wolves in sheep's clothing. People were dying slowly, mentally, and physically. Because the Body of Christ had got so far off God was weeping because those who say they loved him and trusted him were the ones that were hurting him. They were piercing his heart all over again from their actions. Instead of being the examples, they were being the distractions. Pastors were becoming people Gods (People was worshipping them more than HIM) and the church was no longer church but a business and entertainment. People were letting their minds lead them instead of their hearts.

The real prophets that were called were scared to use their prophetic voice to sync the body back together and speak to the atmosphere and command everything to line up according to God's will. Instead, everyone was concerned with money and fame. Everyone was trying to become the **NEXT BIG THING AND THE NEW NEXT!!** Because of this God didn't cause it but he **ALLOWED** a pandemic to hit the land that families and people had to go back to their first love which was him and family. This pandemic made everything shut down. People who worshiped a building (the four walls of a church) and a person (as their God) had no choice but to depend on what was in their heart. This pandemic caused everyone to shift their focus. That making a weekly trip to church (the four walls of a building) doesn't make us save and right. But it's about **BECOMING** the church, an actual place where JESUS lives. Families started loving each other again because they were forced to spend so much time together. People got to meet their neighbors and slow down and rest. They had to rest and try and figure this thing called life out. Some people lost their lives from the pandemic from the Covid-19 literally and then some lost their life mentally because they didn't know how to handle being forced to stay in the home for a long period of time. This is what the world had turned to. People couldn't or didn't know how to work from home and be around their family. They were being drained from having to stay in the house and not being able to get back to what they call their regular life with being around others for a long period of time that had become their family outside of their real family. People didn't realize that they had got so dependent on their everyday fast and popcorn/microwave life that they couldn't function outside of it. No one wasn't fasting and praying anymore as they use to in the past, years and years ago. No one was studying the bible like they use to. And because what they were feeding was leading their life they mentally couldn't shift. They were stuck and trapped. The word says, "**23** The steps of a good man are ordered by the Lord: and he delighted in his way." **Psalm 37:23**. The world wanted to get back to a new normal but what was happening was repentance needed to first come to the church and for the land to **(19 REPENT, THEN, AND TURN TO GOD, SO THAT YOUR SINS MAY BE WIPED OUT, THAT TIMES OF REFRESHING MAY COME FROM THE LORD.) Acts 3:19** NIV. It was deeper than what a natural eye can see. During the pandemic, God was purifying the church first. He was cleaning and purging. No one title, money, or status meant nothing during this pandemic. Everyone was equal and the virus that was going around showed no discrimination. The virus revealed the real from the fake in every area of people's lives. It exposed people for who they were and striped everyone down to a vulnerable state so that God can create and build them into the person he called them to be if they were willing to accept him. And because everyone was equal everyone needed of the same thing...**GOD'S MERCY!!** See people were looking for HOPE...For Something and because of this God started cleansing & purifying the church again. **7** Surely the Lord God will do nothing, but he revealeth his secret unto his servants the prophets. **Amos 3:7**. Again, it takes a prophetic voice to sync the body. Where are the ones walking in The Office of a Prophet?

Jaylnn – People had lost faith in God because of things seen and unseen that happened to them or those around them. In other words, as we say it in the world, life had given us lemons, and many didn't know how to turn it into lemonade. And this is how the cracks in the foundation started. So many find themselves asking if God is good as we say, then why is so much bad stuff happening?

All I'm going to say is, people must realize God's mercy matters because it is what joins us all together despite our differences. So, we are now in a time where we need God's grace because it's a gift we don't deserve, while mercy is where we not getting the punishment we deserve. See we allowed Satan to send a spirit of division among us today. He knows that a house divided against itself will fall, he also knows that if we all come together in unity of faith, we'll arrive at the full stature of Jesus Christ. [13] Till we all come in the unity of the faith, and of the knowledge of the Son of God, unto a perfect man, unto the measure of the stature of the fulness of Christ. **Ephesians 4:13**. So, he has assigned a spirit of division and distraction to operate in our personal lives, our church lives. His goal is to kill, steal and destroy…to bring envying, strife, division and to stunt our spiritual growth. [10] The thief cometh not, but for to steal, and to kill, and to destroy: I am come that they might have life, and that they might have it abundantly. **John 10:10**.

Janiã - The body of Christ has become broken and God is calling for us to come together as one. Too many people are getting away with becoming spiritual Lone Rangers and don't have any accountability. [21] Ye cannot drink the cup of the Lord, and the cup of devils: ye cannot be partakers of the Lord's table, and of the table of devils. **1 Corinthians 10:21**.

We must learn that covering and accountability are not the same. Because you are part of a church you may have spiritual covering, however, accountability is when we have a personal relationship with people who can and do speak into our hearts, our circumstances, relationships, and our lives. They pray for you and cover you. [17] Obey them that have the rule over you, and submit yourselves: for they watch for your souls, as they that must give account, that they may do it with joy, and not with grief: for that is unprofitable for you. **Hebrews 13:17**. Now the flip side to this is we do have "spiritual leaders" in the Body of Christ who think their responsibility is to control the people instead of empowering and uplifting and steering them in the direction of their God-given mandate. Such leaders use manipulation and fear to get their members or flock to do what is needed. This is a form of witchcraft and many don't even know it. Don't get me wrong there's no such thing as a perfect leader or a perfect church because if it was then they would be JESUS. But a true spiritual parent (father or mother) will always include the fulfillment of their people's dreams as part of their primary mission from God.

Chapter 5   God's Power in Your Weakness

Jaylnn – Something's hit within our church and I'm not talking about the pandemic that was going on in the world. Things that weren't of God and people's betrayal was hard. It took me to learn that people didn't change, it was the mask that fell off them. The megachurch that we had was no longer. Had me wondering where God is. Why can't I hear him in this? I know Gods' word (" ⁶ Be strong and of a good courage, fear not, nor be afraid of them: for the LORD thy God, he it is that doth go with thee; he will not fail thee, nor forsake thee.") **Deuteronomy 31:6.** For a minute I was wondering how God will allow us to attach ourselves to people that he knew was only using us as an opportunist when all we did was love people. How do I love God and believe him when I can't even trace him? We kept going on with church as usual and I'm happy that at a time that was hard for my family, that my mom and sisters decided to visit our church. I felt at least I know even through unspoken words that were never said that my family loved my family and wanted to be there to see us through and wasn't looking for anything in return. Plus, I missed them.

This taught me to let God be God. And trust Him even in my adversity that whatever was happening was for the greater purpose of him.

Jazzie – Originally, I started visiting my sister's church and it was only supposed to be an occasional thing. I don't know why God had me to walk away from my assignment within several visits as the head of music at the church I attended to join my sister's family church. Who leaves a place where you had fame, money (a six-figure salary) …I had it all? I could live life and do as I please and no one would say anything or question me. I was free to date whomever I wanted even though I was married and could come and go as I please as long as I showed up for my obligations and kept the people coming in with the music and theatrics. My life was just…that my life. No spiritual accountability whatsoever. However, I obeyed God because I do know that if God asks me to do it, he has a reason-and-a promise-that will break through all my excuses and why's. (²⁶ For ye see your calling, brethren, how that not many wise men after the flesh, not many mighty, not many noble, are called: ²⁷ But God hath chosen the foolish things of the world to confound the wise; and God hath chosen the weak things of the world to confound the things which are mighty; ²⁸ And base things of the world, and things which are despised, hath God chosen, yea, and things which are not, to bring to nought things that are: ²⁹ That no flesh should glory in his presence.) **1 Corinthians 1: 26-29**.

Janiã - My greatest weakness in life was fear. Growing up I never faced the same problems or dealt with the struggles that many dealt with. Alcohol, drugs, homosexuality, sex, in general, was never my struggle or reason for not doing God's will. I always had a fear that I wasn't good enough or looked good enough when many would have killed for my looks. However, my fear stemmed from being molested as a child and trying to cover it up by staying to myself and becoming with many calls or would see as a loner. It gave me pleasure just to see my family safe and happy. I didn't realize until I started visiting my sister's family church that I had suppressed the molestations and had bottled up all the feelings that I had inside. Didn't realize that this hindered me to love my husband and children as I should. Don't get me wrong I know they felt loved, but they didn't have a hundred percent of me because I didn't have a hundred percent to give. I was broken and didn't even realize I was broken. Whatever I did in life I always wanted to stay and operate behind the scene. Because of this I ate and gained weight and used this as an excuse why a lot of stuff I didn't do or participate in. When I start visiting the church, I joined because it just felt right even though I told myself I would never join another church or go regularly. My brother-in-love taught me to take the mask off and stop pretending to have it all together and be honest to myself. He reminded me that God loves to use weak people and for me to depend on God and God only. (**"9** And he said unto me, My grace is sufficient for thee: for my strength is made perfect in weakness. Most gladly therefore will I rather glory in my infirmities, that the power of Christ may rest upon me.) **2 Corinthians 12:9**.

Chapter 6   Restoring Broken Fellowship

Janiã - As I began to meditate, I come to realize that the reason that most people and myself included is broken and it's not because of anything God has done, but because of what we have done as humans. We as humans have let our flesh turn us away from God's standards and made our path and rules in life. We as Christians or the body of Christ have deviated for from God's standard of holiness. It has got to the point that our behavior not only harms others, but our actions have become harmful to ourselves. As a result of sin and living life as we call it, we have rejected God and now put ourselves in His place. This means that sin is not only the fact of our separation from God but also involves our willful disobedience.

Once I realized this, I was no longer confined by the walls that I had built for myself. I learned I was trying to save and influence the world then how can you save the world by trying to be like the world? I started following my passion and it led me to my purpose in God.

First, we must get a relationship with God again in to heal the family and community then maybe we can save the world. How we do this is we have to get our emotions in place. Because a breakup whether it's from a divorce, death or simply growing apart or whatever the cause may be is painful and can destroy a person's self-identity, relations with others, and relationship with God. See a lot of people left or stop going to church and lost faith because of what they call church hurt. But the church didn't hurt them because the church is just a building. Hurt people...hurt them. How we forgot that the church was created to be a safe place where the believers came together and worship, and for healing and to get refueled. But because we allowed a spirit to creep into the body of Christ the authenticity that we once operated in has been diminished in its power. As of now the Body of Christ must come back together in unity. Under the covering of GOD and let's not forget the BLOOD of JESUS and truly heal from the inside out. Now to do this we bust get back a true and authentic relationship with God...OUR FATHER. This is where fasting and praying come into play as we have done in the past. Fasting is a cleanse and it helps cleanse the soul from focusing on blame, regret, confusion, guilt, and shame. Fasting will help you give it all over to God. Fasting is the way that the saints of God received a breakthrough to direct them and help them deal with a crisis in their lives. The conversations with the Lord while fasting are priceless.

(23 Therefore if thou bring thy gift to the altar, and there rememberest that thy brother hath ought against thee; 24 Leave there thy gift before the altar, and go they way; first be reconciled to they brother, and then come and offer thy gift.) **Matthew 5:24**.

Jaylnn – The verse that sticks in my head in Restoring Broken Fellowship is **Romans 12:18** GNT (¹⁸ Do everything possible on your part to live in peace with everybody.)

Reconciliation with my family came when we focused on our relationship and not focused on the problem. See the problem lose it significance and it became irrelevant. "If someone say or tells you that you hurt them, you don't get to decide that you didn't. We learned that it's three sides to every story. Many say two but it's three. It's your side, their side (the other person), and the truth. How you perceived something may not be how it was intended. Could it be a simple misunderstanding? Once we sat down and had a discussion not to see who was right but to find out what is right. Healing took place.

Jazzie – The body of Christ had to remember that Love is an attribute of God. And that Love is how God interacts with us. The best and most beautiful things in this world cannot be seen or even heard but must be felt with the heart. **1 John 4:8 and 16** state that "⁸ He that loveth not knoweth not God; for God is love.; ¹⁶ And we have known and believed that love that God hath to us. God is love; and he that dwelleth in love dwelleth in God, and God in him.

Each of us together shows all of God's graces to the world. No one is perfect. We all sin, but each of us has a purpose here on Earth to show aspects of God to those around us and when we come together in fellowship it is demonstrating God. So, with **Restoring Broken Fellowship Requires Repentance and it needs to start with the Body of Christ because they don't hold any weight anymore. The church lost its authenticity and unity. Let's grow together as one in Christ!**

[4] Nevertheless I have somewhat against thee, because thou hast left thy first love. [5] Remember therefore from whence thou art fallen, and repent, and do the first works; or else I will come unto thee quickly, and will remove thy candlestick out of place, except thou repent. **Revelation 2:4-5**.

[30] And the times of this ignorance God winked at; but now commandeth all men everywhere to repent: [31] Because he appointed a day, in the which he will judge the world righteousness by that man whom he hath ordained; whereof he hath given assurance unto all men, in the hath raised him from the dead. **Acts 17:30-31.**

We as Christian or believers must get back to turning our focus on Christ and His desires and goals for us. We have to get back to remembering that God's Kingdom is not of this world " [36] Jesus answered, My Kingdom is not of this world: if my kingdom were of this world, then would my servants fight, that I should not be delivered to the Jews: but now is my kingdom not from hence. **James 18:36**. We can have friendships and relationships with unbelievers, but true Christian fellowship can only occur within the body of Christ. We are united to one another by common beliefs, purposes, and goals. [3] Can two walk together, except they be agreed? **Amos 3:3**.

[29] For whom he did foreknow, he also did predestinate to be conformed to the image of his Son, that he might be the firstborn among many brethren. [30] Moreover whom he did predestinate, them he also called: and whom he called, them he also justified: and whom he justified, them he also glorified. Romans **8:29-30**.

Chapter 7   Experiencing Life Together

Jaylnn – Through it, all, being with my family and worshiping God together was a great feeling. My family had been keeping every stone that people thought they were throwing at us to hurt us, but what they didn't know they were helping us build a cathedral fit for kings and queens to worship God in truth. Having my family around that genuinely loved me, taught me that everyone that was **CONNECTED** to me might not be **COMMITTED TO ME** and I had to learn the difference. It felt good to have someone watch your back and keep you uplifted and covered while you covered others. And to think they did it for nothing without even being asked. I can say it was great having pillars in the church and not even realizing it. I came to realize I just had to trust the process. While trusting the process I didn't realize that God was building my character, my faith, and my ability to do what he called me to do. A process is a series of actions or steps taken to achieve a particular end. God knew that the temporary separation from my family needed to happen for me to be an effective leader. I had to endure the separation. [16] Confess your faults one to another, and pray one for another, that ye may be healed. The effectual fervent prayer of a righteous man availeth much. **James 5:16**.

One thing as a leader my husband helped me to realize that God does everything for a reason and life is meant to be shared. During the separation from my family, God had taught me that there is a difference between trust and forgiveness. Forgiveness is letting go of the past. Trust has to do with future behavior. Somehow through this whole process growing up, I learned that my expectation of what a family was supposed to be like or what I desired had me stuck in this superficial family lifestyle of beliefs. What I learned when I married and had my own family was to teach my children authenticity. Authenticity for my family was teaching my children to recognize and trust their feelings, good and bad, and act in a way that is consistent with their values and beliefs. By exposing my children to all of life's ups and downs, teaching them how to be emotionally honest with themselves, I believe will give them a great advantage to be prepared for this thing call life. This experience of going through taught me how to genuinely love God's people and how to be forgiving of others. Saying this all the pain and distractions were all necessary and worth it.

The devil intended on keeping us separate but LOVE brought us back together. Jesus commanded us to love. [17] "These things I command you, that ye love one another". **John 15:17**. If you build your life on Love, even the most violent storms of this world will be unable to shake you and keep you down. If you build your family on love, you can win back those that the devil has stolen from you. If you build your business on love, you'll prosper beyond your wildest dreams. See when love rules, prosperity can flow! **LOVE WINS** because God is love. [7] Beloved, let us love one another: for love is of God; and every one that loveth is born of God, and knoweth God. [8] He that loveth not knoweth not God; for God is love. **1 John 4:7-8**. See wherever love is there is also Wealth and Success. The bible says: [3] The Lord hath appeared of old unto me, saying, Yea, I have loved thee with an everlasting love: therefore, with loving kindness have I drawn thee. **Jeremiah 31:3**. Love has become the missing key.

See God needed each one of us healed and with a testimony that would help build his kingdom. His desire was for each one of us to use our unique abilities, talents, and gifts to benefit others, not ourselves. So that's why we went through what we went through.

Jazzie – Forgiveness takes courage. Courage to trust people again from pain from things that I felt happened and things that I felt should have been handled a different way. I had to make a conscious decision to forgive whatever happened in the past that caused the separation in my family. With saying this I had to release the past and live in the present moment and just show up and be there. Be there for wherever I was needed. My family as a whole chose to not be a victim of what society sees as a dysfunctional family anymore. I realize God has always given us choices, so we must choose better once we agree to forgive. We had to write a new story for our family and start making new Godly experiences one at a time. And I can say this is a great feeling to be a loving family again and better than I can remember growing up.

Janiã – It was great that God had given each one of my family members different anointings, gifts, and talents. Talents that were meant to be combined and used for His works to help upbuild the kingdom once we were ready to handle whatever calling he had appointed on our life. **Psalm 133:1** "Behold, how good and how pleasant it is for brethren to dwell together in unity"! The separation helped us get a sense of loyalty and devotion towards one another. Though others saw it as bad, the separation gave each one of us time to grow as an individual and into who God had called us to be. We didn't realize we were each other's crutch and was codependent on each other in some type of way. I realize that my entire life was based around pleasing other people or being their enabler. Now we set back and realize the reason the breakup and division were so harsh because we were such a close unit that the breakup was necessary and nothing else would have separated us.

With saying all this I had to remember that we as the women of the house control the thermostat, so we must set the atmosphere of the house of your family. So, I had to remember to keep my peace I had to start back encouraging myself and speaking affirmations over myself and my life daily. I had to command my morning every day.

Chapter 8   More Than Enough

Janiã – I finally have gotten my life together with God and realize that it takes a total of 360 degrees to make a full circle. Even though I had lost almost everything in a year, my marriage was on a verge of a divorce, my family and everything as I knew it was chaotic, I felt great even in the chaos because I became the woman that God created me to be. I had to lose myself as I knew myself to find myself again and to see myself as God saw me. I had to die to myself just to walk into my God-given call. I had to be ok and not afraid of losing people, but being afraid of losing myself again by trying to please everyone around me. I had to make a conscious decision, that hurt my heart, but it healed my soul. In the mix of learning to love me, I started a business which I enjoyed, which became a multi-million-dollar business and it felt great to help others again in the process. In the process while learning, I had also won the lottery several times, Fantasy Five and the big game for 373 million, so I had more money than I ever dreamed of. People thought I was crazy for allowing folks that walked out of my life to come back in, and people that weren't there for me only for what I can do for them, why was I even entertaining them….They didn't understand it was all part of Gods' plan. He is the Master Puppeteer. And you must let people play their part in this story call life. Those that were meant to be was still connected to me and those that weren't God removed them. Now with all the houses, money and cars, something is still missing, so now tell me what is **MORE THAN ENOUGH?**

Jaylnn – I'm glad that God had done just as he said. I went through so much in life to get to where I am now. I had to learn that some people I thought genuinely loved me and my family only needed us to get ahead. They used us as a platform that nearly broke our hearts because it made us scared to trust people again. Yes, we have the gift of discernment, but we are still human. And yes, some things we could and should have handled a different way, but we all are still learning daily in this thing call life. We must remember this that a pastor once said in his sermon...You must **learn, unlearn**, then **relearn**! Hey, that's the life cycle. The lies, deceit, and betrayal helped our ministry. People came to be nosey and out of human nature curiosity...but left being healed, delivered, and set free. We outgrew the church that we were currently in and had to build a cathedral. Because of everything we went through we were able to start several ministries all around the world to uplift and bring people's hearts back to God. My family and our ministry gave people hope again. Because we didn't fold in our adversity, and we didn't compromise we just stood still on God's word it helped people to have faith one more time. It helped people to see that not all ministries are out to take and scam people out of money that some are here to help and spread the word of the Lord. So, I learned those who betrayed us was part of God's plan to get me and my family to **MORE THAN ENOUGH**!

Jazzie – I had to ask myself is what I'm doing inside of the church and assisting my sister in ministry is getting me closer to where I want to be? Is it getting me closer to where God wants me? I learned in going through, what all I went through that my family had to get back to the basics, and once we did that it was going to strengthen the foundation again. See I already experience wealth and being head of a top company and being famous in ministry before so this wouldn't fulfill me. The money wouldn't be enough. See I had to de-clutter my life from all complications and superficialities and reconnect with my core values of life. I had to decide what was important to me. Once I did this it reunited and rekindled my marriage and strengthen my bond with my family and to me, this is **MORE THAN ENOUGH**!

Prayer and Words of Encouragement

My prayer is for the loss to return to a pure place. A place of truth, honesty, kindness, love, and unity. In the bible it says, "Blessed are the pure in heart, for they shall see God", because the heart sees beyond the intellect. I need everyone to know no matter how far you think you are from God, that there is NO distance in spirit. I encourage everyone to block out the noise of frustration, disappointments, and betrayal. But walk in strength, knowledge, and truth. Remember God is just waiting on you to return to him with open arms…..**So, let's turn our hearts back to GOD**.

ABOUT THE AUTHOR

Frankie Lafaye Dumas-Harrison (a.k.a.- Faye) is married to Clay Harrison and together they have raised seven children. She is an influencer, reformer, graphic artist, brand strategist and she is an upcoming inspiring author. She is the proud owner of Frankie Dumas-Harrison LLC dba-Professional Outlook.net. In her spare time, she is an avid reader and she loves motivating and assisting others.

Before she started pursing her desires to write she serves as the Senior Admin Coordinator Admin at GSU (Business Services/Purchasing Dept) for over 22 yrs. She is known to be altruistic which has become her greatest attribute.

She lives by the saying **"EMPOWERING OTHERS TO DREAM AGAIN"**

Let's connect:

IG - @faye_dumas

FB – Frankie Dumas-Harrison

www.professionaloutlook.net

www.frankiedumasharrison.com

COMING SOON!

MORE THAN ENOUGH!

By: Faye Dumas-Harrison